THE FOX WISH

BY Kimiko Aman

ILLUSTRATED BY Komako Sakai

chronicle books · san francisco

It was right in the middle of snack that I remembered.

I'd left my jump rope at the park!

"Where are you going?" Lukie asked.

"I have to go," I told him. "You can come, too."

But there wasn't anything hanging from the tree branch where I'd left it.

Where could it be?

A big wind blew.

"What's that?" Lukie asked.

From somewhere nearby we could hear other kids laughing.

"That sounds like Thomas and Samantha," I told him.

"Let's go."

"Come on, Lukie," I said.
"It's coming from over there."

The laughs were louder now, and I could hear it:

the *swish, whip* of the jump rope.

But it wasn't Thomas and
Samantha jump-roping.

It was foxes.

"Doxy, foxy,
touch the ground.

Doxy, foxy,
turn around.

Turn to the east,
and turn to the west,

and choose the one that
you like best."

The foxes were not very good at jump rope.
They were good jumpers, but their tails kept getting
caught in the rope.

It didn't seem polite to laugh at them, even though they looked so funny. But Lukie couldn't help it.

At that, the foxes dropped the rope.

"What was that?"
asked the smallest one.

It didn't seem polite to spy on them either, so we tiptoed out from the tree's shadow.

"Hi," I said.

"Oh, thank heavens!" said a fox. "By any chance might you be able to teach us how to jump rope without tripping?"

What a silly bunch. "Well, just keep your tail straight up your back," I told them. "Like this."

Of course their jump-roping skills improved immediately.

"You're doing it!" I said.

"What fun!" said the fox.

"Hooray!" said Lukie.

When it was my time to turn, I double-checked. Just as I'd guessed,

it was my missing jump rope.

My name was right on the handle where I'd painted it.

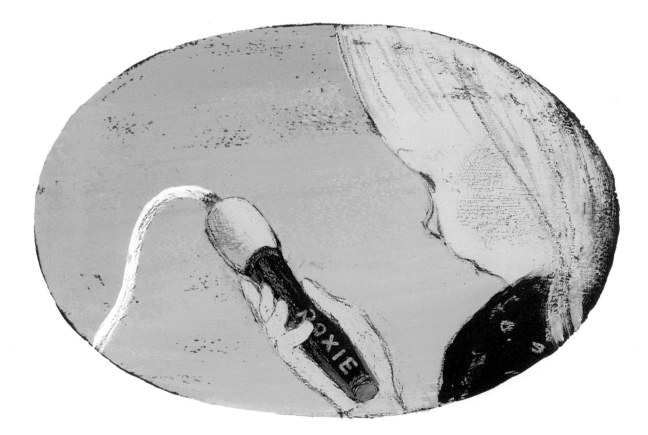

Soon the sky was peachy, and we couldn't see enough to jump.

"It's time to go home," Lukie told me.

But as I crouched to pick up my rope, the smallest fox bounded over.
"This is mine," she told us. "On our way here, remember Moxie?
You heard me, I said, I just wish we had a game to play—"

Moxie nodded.

"—and then, when we came to this nice clearing a ways back, well,
this rope was just hanging there, from a branch, with my name on it
and everything, just a little wish come true!

Have you ever heard of a luckier day?

I should wish for a thousand wishes!"

"Your name is Roxie?" I asked.

"But!" Lukie said. "That's my sister's name—"

I shushed him.

"It's okay, Lukie. Roxie, you're the best jump-roper I've ever seen. Do you want to maybe play together again someday?"

"I'll wish for it!" Roxie told us, and she darted away, the jump rope in her teeth.

Lukie and I were quiet all the way back through the park.
The light was golden and the air was warm, and in our footsteps
I kept hearing the rhythm of the jump-rope rhyme.

"Can we do that again, Rox?" Lukie asked me. The happy face
of Roxie the fox popped into my head.

"Sure, Lukie," I told him. "I like watching wishes come true."

Then I wished to race him home,

and he wished to win.

First published in the United States of America in 2017 by Chronicle Books LLC.

Originally published in Japan in 2003 under the title *Kitsune no Kamisama* by POPLAR Publishing Co., Ltd., Tokyo.

English translation rights arranged with POPLAR Publishing Co., Ltd. through Japan Foreign-Rights Centre.

Text copyright © 2003 by Kimiko Aman.

Illustrations copyright © 2003 by Komako Sakai.

Library of Congress Cataloging-in-Publication Data available.

ISBN 978-1-4521-5188-5

Manufactured in China.

Design by Michelle Clement.
Typeset in Brandon Text and Blog Script. The illustrations in this book were rendered in paper, acrylic gouache, oil pencil, and ballpoint pen.

10 9 8 7 6 5 4 3 2

Chronicle Books LLC
680 Second Street
San Francisco, California 94107

Chronicle Books—we see things differently.
Become part of our community at www.chroniclekids.com.